MW01250781

Travel

Kay Robertson

rourkeeducationalmedia.com

www.rourkeeducationalmedia.com

PHOTO CREDITS: Cover; ©; NASA Photo, 4; © mbbirdy, 5; © zorani, 6; © Warren Goldswain, 7; © Brocreative, 9; © iceninephoto, pamelajane, 10; © Nejron Photo / Shutterstock.com, 11; © zirconicusso / Shutterstock.com, 12; © Kativ, 13; © ssuaphoto, 14; © Grafissimo, 15; © Grafissimo, 16; © Konstantin Sutyagin, YinYang 17; © bigapple, jacomstephens, 18; © studioworxx, Rudy Balasko, 19; © ryasick, 20; © ryasick, 21; ©   solid-istanbul, 22; © hfng, 23; © Christian Mueller, 24; © Jag_cz, 25; ©   solid-istanbul, 26; © felix140800, 27; © Previous book, 28; © prawny, Ruth Peterkin 29; © Maytals, microgen, 30; © Andrea Danti, 31; © Previous book, 32; © Kuzma, © Nobilior, 33; Roman Sakhno, 34; © Oko Laa, 35; © skinman, pixelete.com, 36; © skinman, 41; © NASA Photo, U.S Air Force, 38; © Reaction Engines Ltd., NASA, MSFC, 39; © Bristol Space Planes, 40; © 21stcentech, 42; © Devonyu, 43; © pixelparticle

Edited by: Precious McKenzie

Cover by: Tara Raymo
Interior design by: Cory Davis

Library of Congress PCN Data

STEM Guides to Travel / Kay Robertson.
    p. cm. -- (STEM Everyday)
Includes index.
ISBN 978-1-62169-848-7 (hardcover)
ISBN 978-1-62169-743-5 (softcover)
ISBN 978-1-62169-951-4 (e-Book)
Library of Congress Control Number: 2013936453

Also Available as:
ROURKE'S
e-Books

Rourke Educational Media
Printed in the United States of America,
North Mankato, Minnesota

Rourke

rourkeeducationalmedia.com

customerservice@rourkeeducationalmedia.com • PO Box 643328 Vero Beach, Florida 32964

Table of Contents

Introduction

What does the word **travel** mean to you? Traveling is something people do all the time, both in small and big ways.

A means of traveling, or getting from one place to another, is a form of **transportation**.

Can you name a few forms of transportation? Probably the ones that spring to mind are cars, trains, and planes. For instance, when you take the bus to school, you are traveling. But did you know that **escalators** are also a form of transportation? Of course, escalators don't take you very far, but they still move you from one place to another.

The width and speed of the escalator determine how many people an escalator can carry per minute. A narrow escalator moving at 1.5 feet (.45 meters) per second can carry about 34 people per minute.

In this book, you're going to learn about different types of transportation. You will also learn about the differences between these types of transportation.

You see, not all forms of transportation are equal. The key difference between forms of transportation is **speed**, in other words, what method of travel will get you to your destination the quickest. To figure out the fastest way to get from one place to another, you are going to use math to compare the different forms of transportation.

What would you guess is the slowest form of transportation?

Probably the slowest form of transportation is something you do every day, walking!

Did you know that when you walk from one classroom to another you are using a form of transportation?

Take A Walk

When was the last time you took a nice, long walk?

These days, walking is generally thought of as a form of **recreation** or **exercise**. But actually, walking is the most basic form of transportation people have. In fact, walking is the one form of transportation a person can take advantage of without needing any other equipment.

Stride length varies from person to person. One way to measure your exact stride length is to set a distance, 10 feet (3 meters), for instance, and see how many steps it takes you to walk that length.

Walking is no longer considered a serious form of transportation simply because we have many other, far more **efficient**, ways to travel from one place to another. Cars, trains, and planes are all faster than walking.

This has probably raised an interesting question in your mind. Just how fast is walking?

The first thing to do would be to find out how many steps you take in one minute. You will need to use a stopwatch or some other form of timer to do this.

Using this information, can you calculate how long it would take you to walk one mile?

The mile is the basis of length in the U.S. Customary System of measurement, also known as the Imperial System of measurement.

STEM in Action

Let's say that you took 60 steps in one minute. What this means will become clearer when you multiply 60 by 2. The 2 stands for two feet. This is the **average** stride length, or the distance a person covers with a single step.

$$60 \times 2 = 120$$

Now you know that in one minute you walk a distance of roughly 120 feet.

One mile is equal to roughly 5,280 feet. If you walk at a pace of about 120 feet per minute, you can find out how long it would take you to travel a mile by using division:

$$5{,}280 \div 120 = 44$$

So, to walk a distance of one mile, it would take you about 44 minutes.

What if your destination, the place you have to go, is 20 miles away? How long would it take you to get there by walking?

You can find out by multiplying the time it takes to travel one mile by the number of miles:

$$20 \times 44 = 880$$

It would take about 880 minutes to travel a distance of 20 miles on foot. To convert that number to hours, you can divide it by 60, which is the number of minutes in one hour:

$$880 \div 60 = 14.6$$

Wow! To walk a distance of 20 miles would take about 15 hours!

When you realize the length of time it takes to walk one mile, it makes sense that people worked to develop easier, more efficient forms of travel. The relatively slow speed of walking led to the invention of the form of transport you are probably most familiar with, the automobile.

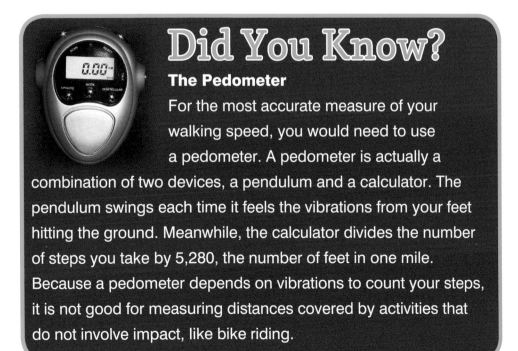

Did You Know?

The Pedometer

For the most accurate measure of your walking speed, you would need to use a pedometer. A pedometer is actually a combination of two devices, a pendulum and a calculator. The pendulum swings each time it feels the vibrations from your feet hitting the ground. Meanwhile, the calculator divides the number of steps you take by 5,280, the number of feet in one mile. Because a pedometer depends on vibrations to count your steps, it is not good for measuring distances covered by activities that do not involve impact, like bike riding.

Using A Speedometer

Have you ever looked at the **dashboard** of your family's car? Maybe you have seen it from the passenger's seat on the right, but have you ever sat behind the driver's seat?

When you learn to drive, the speedometer is the instrument on the instrument panel of your car that you will check the most. If you're not aware of your speed, you could end up with a speeding ticket!

The numbers we're interested in are located on an instrument just above the steering wheel. This particular instrument is called a **speedometer**. As you may have guessed, a speedometer is used to tell the speed at which a car is traveling.

Your speedometer will have a series of numbers that look something like this: 20 40 60 80 100 120. Obviously, these are not your standard 1, 2, 3, 4 numbers. The labeled numbers on a speedometer are **multiples**. To be precise, they are multiples of twenty:

$$0 \times 20 = 0$$
$$1 \times 20 = 20$$
$$2 \times 20 = 40$$
$$3 \times 20 = 60$$
$$4 \times 20 = 80$$
$$5 \times 20 = 100$$

You have already dealt with multiples if you have ever practiced your **multiplication** tables. For example, have you ever done multiples of 5? Try it now:

$$0 \times 5 = 0$$
$$1 \times 5 = 5$$
$$2 \times 5 = 10$$
$$3 \times 5 = 15$$
$$4 \times 5 = 20$$

Note that the labeled numbers on a speedometer are multiples of 20. That is because a speedometer also contains a lot of invisible numbers. Take a closer look at the speedometer. For instance, between 20 and 40 there are some lines, or **notches**, that are not given numbers. What do they represent?

It's really very simple. Just as the labeled numbers are multiples of 20, the notches that are not labeled are multiples of 5. So, in between 20 and 40 are three hidden numbers: 25, 30, and 35.

Another way to look at a speedometer is to say that each notch is a multiple of 5, but only the multiples of 20 are labeled. Speedometers are set up this way for convenience. If a speedometer included every single number from 0 to 120, it would have to be pretty big, and it would be very hard to read!

Did You Know?

A gear odometer registers one mile (1.61 kilometers) after spinning 1,690 times. Can you calculate how many times the gear of an odometer would spin for a trip of 15 miles (24.14 kilometers)?

Speedometer

Odometer

STEM Fast Fact !

The Odometer

Within the speedometer can be found another device called an odometer. The purpose of the odometer is to measure the number of miles a vehicle travels in its lifetime. It is illegal to **reset** a vehicle's odometer. Although digital, or computerized, odometers are becoming more popular, old-fashioned gear odometers are still very common.

Understanding Miles Per Hour

In the last section, you started to learn about the numbers on a speedometer. In this section, you're going to learn about what those numbers mean.

If you look closely at the speedometer again, you'll see that it is labeled not only with numbers, but letters. Somewhere on the speedometer you will find letters that read mph. Perhaps you know already that these letters stand for miles per hour.

Miles per hour is a unit of measurement much like the feet per minute calculation you did in the section on walking. Of course, a car covers a much greater distance in a shorter period of time than a person walking, which is why the standard is miles per hour, rather than feet per minute.

STEM in Action ?

Let's calculate how long it would take to travel 20 miles. You'll be in a car traveling at 20 miles per hour. How long would it take to get to your destination now?

$$20 \div 20 = 1$$

So, in a car traveling at 20 miles per hour, it would take 1 hour to travel a distance of 20 miles.

Try This

If you were in a car traveling at an average speed of 60 mph (96.51 kph), how long would it take you to travel a distance of 1,150 miles (1,851 kilometers)?

$1,150 \div 60 = ?$

It's also important to note that, for the most part, a car can travel much faster than 20 miles per hour. In reality, you could travel a distance of 20 miles in about 15 minutes. That's quite an improvement over the slow pace of walking!

And that is exactly what is meant by the term efficiency. Cars are simply more efficient forms of travel than walking. Cars help people get to where they need to go quickly.

If you were in a car traveling at a speed of 63 mph, how would your speed compare to this speed limit sign?

The speedometer is not only useful for determining how long it will take to get somewhere. It is also an important tool for figuring how the speed of a car being driven compares to the **speed limit** of a stretch of road. Speed limits are not randomly selected. They are chosen because they are thought to be the safest speed for that particular stretch of road. Speed limits can go up and down depending on a number of different factors, including the path of the road, the weather conditions of a particular area, and the population density of the area the road travels through.

For instance, on a **highway** that passes by a stretch of bare land, the speed limit might be 65 mph. In a **residential** area where children might play, a typical speed might be 30 mph.

Policemen also take notice if you are driving too slowly. Slow driving might be safe, but it can be an annoyance to other drivers on the road.

Because speed limits are extremely important for safety, the police will often stop people who are not traveling at a speed close to the speed limit. That is why the speedometer is useful for making sure that you are traveling at the required speed.

STEM in Action ?

What if you are in a car that is traveling 40 miles per hour on a highway with a speed limit of 65 miles per hour? How much slower are you driving compared to the speed limit? To find out, just subtract the smaller number from the larger one.

$$65 - 40 = 25$$

You are traveling about 25 miles per hour below the speed limit.

Let's say you are driving in an area with a speed limit of 30 mph, but the speedometer indicates that you are driving at 45 mph. How many miles per hour over the speed limit are you traveling?

You can find out by using subtraction:

$$45 - 30 = 15$$

You are traveling 15 miles per hour above the speed limit. This kind of behavior, known as speeding, can get you pulled over by the police.

The term horsepower dates back to a time when the power for most forms of transportation was provided by horses.

STEM
Fast Fact !

Horsepower

Another term often applied to cars is horsepower. Horsepower is a unit of measure that was invented by an engineer named James Watt. More specifically, it is a unit for measuring **work**.

A car, for instance, is designed to move, but in order to move, it has to carry its own weight. The heavier a car is, the more work the engine has to do. Horsepower measures the amount of power a car can produce against its own load. High performance cars have a lot of horsepower in relation to their weight. This means that they can speed up more quickly than a car with less horsepower.

Locomotives

At one time, locomotives, or trains, were the most popular form of long-distance travel in America.

Although trains may not be as popular for long-distance travel as they once were, they are very popular with **commuters** traveling short distances. The fact is, a journey by train can often take less time than the same journey by car. This is because a train can reach a greater **average** speed than a car.

Traveling by train is fast, efficient, and inexpensive. Trains are one of the most eco-friendly ways you can travel.

Try This

If this train maintains an average speed of 80 mph, how long will it take to make a trip of 3,750 miles (6,035 kilometers)?

An average is a number that represents a group of numbers. If you are told that a car is traveling at an average speed of 45 mph, that doesn't mean that the car is always traveling at 45 mph. Sometimes it might be traveling faster than 45 mph, sometimes slower. Rather, the idea of average speed is that at any given time the speed of the car is about 45 mph.

A train can often reach a greater average speed than that of a car, partially because there are no obstacles in the way. Remember, there are a lot of cars in the world. Sometimes they get in each others' way, and the result is a traffic jam.

Let's do some math to compare train travel and car travel. Imagine a journey between two cities, Los Angeles, California and Chicago, Illinois. The **approximate** distance between these two cities is 2,000 miles (3,219 kilometers).

Chicago

Los Angeles

25 Hours by Train

30.77 Hours by Car

STEM in Action ?

How much faster is the train to Chicago? You can find out by subtracting the smaller number from the larger number:

$$31 - 25 = 6$$

The same journey by train would take about six hours less. About how long would it take you to travel from Los Angeles to Chicago if you went by car and your average speed was around 65 mph? You can find out by dividing the number of miles (2,000) by the average speed (65 mph):

$$2,000 \div 65 = 30.77$$

So, it would take about 30.77 hours to make that trip by car. Now let's imagine doing that trip on a train with an average speed of 80 mph. How long would the trip from Los Angeles to Chicago take?

$$2,000 \div 80 = 25$$

So, it takes about 31 hours in the car and 25 hours on the train. We can find the difference by subtracting the smaller number from the larger number.

$$31 - 25 = 6$$

It would take 6 less hours to make the trip by train than by car.

STEM in Action ?

Bullet trains are high speed passenger trains that can go as fast as 300 mph. Bullet trains are popular in Asia and Europe.

Remember our trip from Los Angeles to Chicago? We figured out that it would take 25 hours to make the 2,000 mile trip on a traditional train. Now let's see what the difference in the travel time would be if we were taking the same trip on a bullet train.

First, we need to find out how long it would take us to travel 2,000 miles at 300 miles per hour.

$$2{,}000 \div 300 = 6.66$$

Now that we know it would take about 7 hours to make the trip by bullet train, we can find the difference by subtracting the smaller number from the larger number.

$$25 - 7 = 18$$

Wow! You would save 18 hours by traveling on a bullet train.

Along with the time factor, there are many reasons why some people prefer trains to driving. First of all, trains create less pollution than cars and are therefore better for the environment. Trains also require less responsibility. For instance, you can take a nap on a train ride, which is something you absolutely cannot do when you're driving. Likewise, in a car you would have to stop to get something to eat, while many trains have food service.

In terms of speed, though, both trains and cars are left in the dust by planes.

STEM Fast Fact

You are probably already familiar with buses. Maybe you even take one to get to and from school. Unless you live in a big city you might not know that buses are also a common form of **metropolitan** transportation.

Typically, a car can outrun a bus, since a bus has to carry a much greater weight than a car going at a **comparable** speed. And because a city bus is a public service, the bus will stop every few blocks to pick up and drop-off passengers.

Airplanes

Planes are the most popular mode of passenger travel available today. This is largely due to the incredible speed at which travel is possible in a plane. Compared to the time it takes to get somewhere in a train or a car, plane travel takes place in the blink of an eye.

Aviation speed is most often expressed in knots (kt). One knot is one nautical mile per hour. Typical air speed for long distance commercial passenger flights is 475-500 knots.

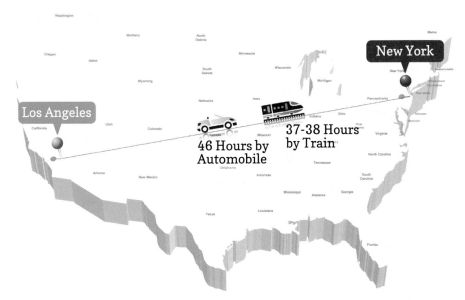

To demonstrate, let's plan another imaginary trip. This time the journey will take you from Los Angeles, California, on the West Coast of the United States, to New York City, New York, on the East Coast of the United States. The distance between these two cities is roughly 3,000 miles (4,828 kilometers).

STEM in Action ?

Calculate how long it would take to make that trip in a car traveling at an average speed of 65 mph:

$$3,000 \div 65 = 46.15$$

So, a journey from Los Angeles to New York City by automobile would take about 46 hours.

Let's pretend that you could travel directly from Los Angeles to New York City in a train going at an average speed of 80 mph. How long would it take to make that journey?

$$3,000 \div 80 = 37.5$$

The journey from Los Angeles to New York City by train would take about 37 to 38 hours, which is a slight improvement over the 46-hour trip by car.

Boeing 747

STEM in Action ?

The trip from Los Angeles to New York City in a plane takes about 41 hours less than the same trip in a car!

For the purposes of this example, imagine that the plane is a Boeing 747 aircraft. A Boeing 747 is capable of an average speed of about 560 mph. How long would it take to fly from Los Angeles to New York City at that speed?

$$3,000 \div 560 = 5.35$$

So, to travel from Los Angeles to New York City in a plane only takes about five hours!

Using these numbers, how much faster is the journey from Los Angeles to New York City by plane compared to a car? To find out, just subtract the smaller number from the larger number:

$$46.15 - 5.35 = 40.8$$

Now let's compare all three of our results:

CAR = 46.15 hours
TRAIN = 37.5 hours
PLANE = 5.35 hours

Now you understand why plane travel is so popular!

Plane travel has other advantages as well. One thing that cars, trains, and even a person on foot can't deal with very well is water. Did you know that water covers about 70 percent of the Earth's surface? When you think about that, the difficulties that water presents for travel becomes obvious. You can't just drive a car or a train through water. And unless you are superhuman, you can't really swim across an entire ocean either.

For planes, water is no problem. They just fly over it. Planes have made fast international travel, travel from one continent to another, possible.

Container ships are cargo ships that carry an entire load in truck size containers. They carry the majority of the world's dry cargo, which doesn't require temperature control.

For a long time, the most popular method of international travel was by boat. Boats are still used today, particularly for shipping purposes.

Planes are simply quicker than boats, mainly because boats experience so much **resistance** from the water. A journey from America to Europe takes days on a boat. A plane can travel that same distance in a matter of hours.

Although planes are very fast, there is still room for improvement. That quest for a faster trip is exactly what led to the development of **supersonic** planes. Supersonic means traveling faster than the speed of sound.

STEM
Fast Fact !

Propellers

The planes you are used to seeing today are mostly jet aircraft. Before jets, planes had propellers.

If your family owns a boat you already know a little about propellers. A propeller is a device that looks like the blade of a fan. As you may have already guessed from the name, a propeller is a machine that propels, or pushes, a craft through a substance like water or air.

Propeller aircraft were slowly replaced because, compared to jet engines, propellers are fairly slow. You can still see propeller aircraft for yourself though, by visiting a museum of transportation or watching old movies. There are still some small propeller planes in use today. And helicopters use propellers, though their propellers are located on the top and in the back instead of out front!

What About Light And Sound?

Sound travels.

It might seem hard to believe, but sound is just waves of air. Unlike water, you can't see air, but it is there. Sound moves at an incredible rate of speed.

How fast is sound? Sound travels at 1,100 feet (335.28 meters) per second.

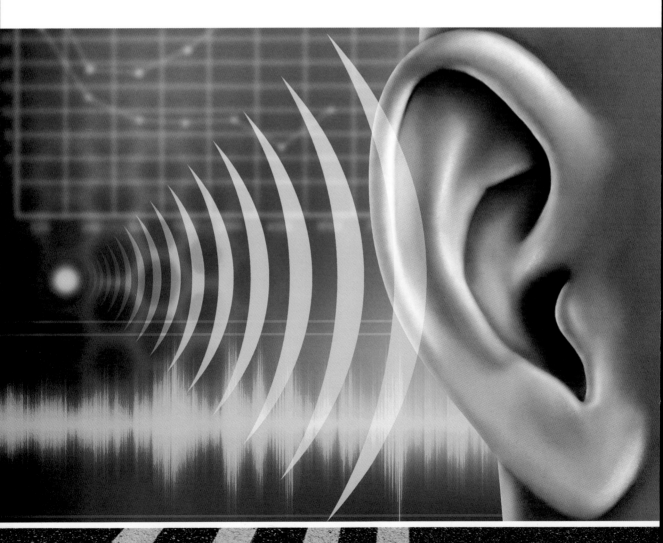

You cannot see sound waves, but they behave in much the same way as the water waves pictured here.

Imagine that you and a friend are standing in a large, open field. You are exactly one mile (1.61 kilometers) apart. If you were to make a loud noise, like the beep of a horn, how long would it take for that sound to reach your friend?

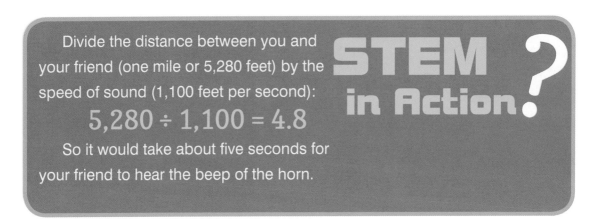

Divide the distance between you and your friend (one mile or 5,280 feet) by the speed of sound (1,100 feet per second):

$$5,280 \div 1,100 = 4.8$$

So it would take about five seconds for your friend to hear the beep of the horn.

STEM in Action?

Even the speed of sound seems slow compared to the speed of light. Light travels at an incredible 186,000 miles (299,792 kilometers) per second!

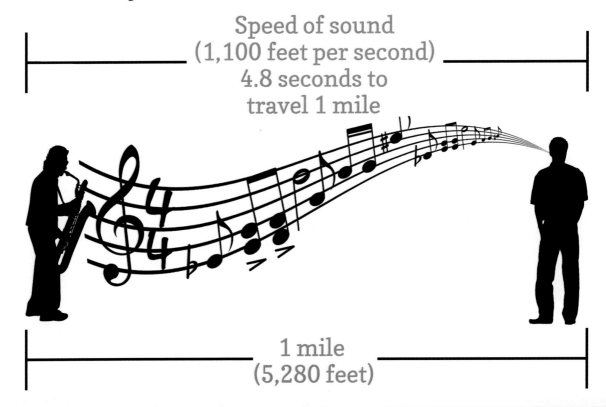

Speed of sound
(1,100 feet per second)
4.8 seconds to
travel 1 mile

1 mile
(5,280 feet)

Try This

It takes about eight minutes for sunlight to reach the earth. If it was 4:30 p.m. when this photo was taken, at what time did the sunlight pictured here begin its journey?

The speed of light might seem impossible. But if you think about it, it happens every day. For instance, the rays of light created by the Sun have to travel to Earth.

How long does it take for the light created by the sun to reach the Earth?

You can find out, but get ready, because you're going to be dealing with some very big numbers here.

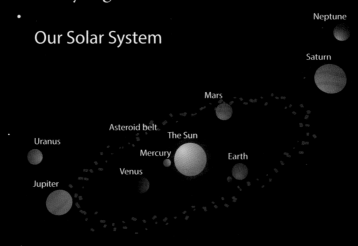

Our Solar System

STEM in Action

The distance from the sun to the Earth is about 93 million miles.

$$93,000,000 \text{ miles}$$

Meanwhile, light travels at 186,000 miles per second. In order to find out how long it takes sunlight to reach the Earth, you have to divide the distance from the sun to the Earth (93,000,000 miles) by the speed of light:

$$93,000,000 \div 186,000 = 500 \text{ seconds}$$

To convert that number into minutes, divide 500 seconds by the number of seconds in one minute (60):

$$500 \div 60 = 8.3$$

Therefore, it takes a little more than eight minutes for a ray of sunlight to travel across space to the Earth!

STEM Fast Fact !

Sonic Boom

When a supersonic aircraft reaches top speed, it produces a sonic boom, a kind of noise produced by the waves of air the aircraft creates.

You already know that sound waves travel in much the same way that water waves do. Have you ever thrown a pebble into a pond? Then you have seen that waves travel in circles. They start from the center of the disturbance and then spread out.

But what happens if waves are created by a craft that is moving faster than the waves themselves? In that case, the craft, for instance a speedboat, creates what is called a wake, or a big, single wave formed by a number of smaller waves. And, since the craft is traveling faster than the waves, the wake actually appears a few seconds after the craft has passed. That is exactly what a sonic boom is. It is the wake created by the airwaves disturbed by a supersonic jet.

Felix Baumgartner, an Austrian skydiver, set a world record in skydiving when he fell at an estimated speed of 843.6 mph (1,357.64 kph) on October 14, 2012.

Space Travel

What kinds of travel will people be able to experience in the future? How much more efficient will those forms of travel be than what we have now? And how can travel speeds possibly improve?

Remember that you learned about two different forms of resistance. Water craft deal with the resistance created by water, while aircraft deal with air resistance. Take away both types of resistance and the potential for faster speeds is incredible.

The reason why the surface of the Earth appears to glow is because of our planet's atmosphere. The atmosphere is what causes wind resistance for planes. By leaving the Earth's atmosphere, space planes will be able to travel at incredible speeds.

Soyuz is the most frequently used launch vehicle in the world. The rocket is assembled and transported horizontally and turned into position before launch.

Faster speeds are the concept behind the space planes, which are considered to be the next big development in travel and transportation. Space planes will actually leave the Earth's atmosphere in order to travel great distances without air resistance. It is estimated that space planes will be capable of travel speeds up to 15 times the speed of sound.

The Skylon is a single-stage-to-orbit vehicle, able to achieve orbit without breaking away from a launch engine.

Boeing X-37

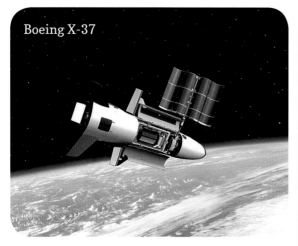

The Boeing X-37 is an unmanned spacecraft. It is boosted into space by a rocket, then it reenters Earth's atmosphere and lands as a single stage-to-orbit space plane.

STEM in Action?

How fast is that?

You can find out by multiplying the speed of sound (1,100 feet per second) by 15:

1,100 x 15 = 16,500

So space planes could potentially travel at speeds up to 16,500 feet per second! Can you find out how many miles per second that is?

16,500 ÷ 5,280 = 3.125

About three miles a second!

Space Planes

The United States Air Force is testing robotic space planes. The highly classified test missions are unmanned.

Ascender

Bristol Spaceplanes Limited

Boeing X-51A Waverider

The United States Air Force and NASA joined forces to develop hypersonic jets, called scramjets. These unmanned jets fly at incredible speeds. The X-43A holds the current record traveling at almost 7,000 miles (11,265 kilometers) per hour.

Scramjet X-43A

Space planes won't be that efficient, though. They'll need extra time to take off and leave the atmosphere. Likewise, reentering the atmosphere will require extra time. Still, even with those factors considered, you're still looking at a journey of about one hour!

STEM in Action ?

How long would it take a space plane, for instance, to travel the journey from New York City to Great Britain?

To find out, you need to divide the number of miles between New York City and Great Britain (3,500) by the number of miles a space plane can cover in one second (3.125):

$$3,500 \div 3.125 = 1,120$$

So a space plane could travel from New York City to Great Britain in about 1,120 seconds.

How many minutes is that?

To find out, divide the number of seconds (1,120) by the number of seconds in one minute (60):

$$1,120 \div 60 = 18$$

Eighteen minutes! Pretty amazing, isn't it?

Conclusion

Have you ever heard the expression, "time is money"? Do you know what it means?

It is a phrase that describes the importance of time in relation to work. The amount of money a person can make is determined by, among other things, how quickly they can do their work.

We live in a fast culture, and it is only getting faster. That is why the quest for ever-faster modes of transportation will continue.

If space planes do become the dominant form of transportation, the only other possible improvement would be some method of **instantaneous** travel. One possibility would be the kind of travel you see in science fiction films, where people are teleported from one location to another by use of lasers that deconstruct and reassemble their bodies. Such a mode of transportation would bring people very close to traveling at the speed of light.

But everyone knows that people can't travel at the speed of light. That's impossible!

True. But people once said that about flying. . . .

You'll just have to wait and see!

Glossary

approximate (uh-PRAHK-suh-mit): not exact, an estimate

average (AV-uh-rij): a number you get by adding a group of numbers together and then dividing the the sum by the number of figures added

commuters (kuh-MYOO-turz): people who travel some distance to work or school, usually by bus, car, or train

comparable (kuhm-PAR-uh-buhl): similar

efficient (i-FISH-uhnt): something that operates without a great deal of waste, expense, or need for effort

instantaneous (in-stuhn-TAY-nee-uhs): instantly, without interruption

metropolitan (met-ruh-PAH-li-tuhn): a city area

multiples (MUHL-tuh-puhlz): the result of multiplying a single number by a series of other numbers

multiplication (MUHL-ti-pli-KAY-shuhn): a method for adding large groups of numbers

notches (nahch-iz): marks or symbols used to represent something like a word or letter

reset (re-SET): to make a machine or program start again from the beginning

resistance (ri-ZIS-tuhns): a force that slows down or prevents motion

speed (speed): distance traveled in a specific amount of time

supersonic (soo-pur-SAH-nik): faster than the speed of sound (1,110 feet per second)

work (wurk): the ability to get something done using energy or ability

Index

Metric System

We actually have two systems of weights and measure in the United States. Quarts, pints, gallons, ounces, and pounds are all units of the U.S. Customary System, also known as the English System.

The other system of measurement, and the only one sanctioned by the United States government, is the metric system, which is also known as the International System of Units. French scientists developed the metric system in the 1790s. The basic unit of measurement in the metric system is the meter, which is about one ten-millionth the distance from the North Pole to the equator.

STEM Fast Fact

Most of the world uses the metric system. In terms of travel, this usually means that distances are measured not in miles, but in kilometers. One mile is equal to 1.621 kilometers.

The calculations for metric measurement are a simple matter of multiplication. For instance, if a distance is 20 miles, how many kilometers is it?

$$1.621 \times 20 = 32.42$$

20 miles is equal to about 32.42 kilometers!

If a car is traveling at 50 mph, how fast is it going in kilometers per hour (kph)?

$$50 \times 1.621 = 81.05$$

The car is traveling a little over 81 kph!

Show What You Know

1. Where did the term horsepower come from? How is it used today?

2. Define miles per hour.

3. If you wanted to travel from New York to California, which would be the fastest way? The slowest?

4. When does a sonic boom happen?

5. If you were given a chance to ride in a space plane, would you do it? What might it feel like? What might you see?

Websites to Visit

www.nasa.gov/centers/dryden/news/FactSheets/FS-016-DFRC.html

www.smm.org/sound/nocss/top.html

www.scholastic.com/browse/article.jsp?id=3754495